KU-759-272

PETER RABBIT'S^{TM}
BEDTIME STORY BOOK

PETER RABBIT'S™
BEDTIME STORY BOOK

FREDERICK WARNE

Published by the Penguin Group

Penguin Books Ltd, 27 Wrights Lane, London W8 5TZ, England

Penguin Putnam Inc., 375 Hudson Street, New York, N.Y. 10014, USA

Penguin Books Australia Ltd, Ringwoood, Victoria, Australia

Penguin Books Canada Ltd, 10 Alcorn Avenue, Toronto, Ontario, Canada M4V 3B2

Penguin Books (NZ) Ltd, Private Bag 102902, NSMC, Aukland, New Zealand

Penguin Books India (P) Ltd, 11 Community Centre, Panchsheel Park, New Delhi 110 017, India

Penguin Books (South Africa) (Pty) Ltd, 5 Watkins Street, Denver Ext 4, 2094, South Africa

Penguin Books Ltd, Registered Offices: Harmondsworth, Middlesex, England

Visit our web site at: www.peterrabbit.com

First published by Frederick Warne 1994
This edition first published 2000

1 3 5 7 9 10 8 6 4 2

Copyright © Frederick Warne, 2000

Illustrations from The World of Peter Rabbit and FriendsTM animated television and video series,
a TV Cartoons Ltd production for Frederick Warne & Co., copyright © Frederick Warne & Co., 1992, 1993, 1994

Original copyright in Beatrix Potter's text and illustrations © Frederick Warne & Co., 1902, 1903, 1904, 1907, 1908,

Frederick Warne & Co. is the owner of all rights, copyrights and trademarks in the Beatrix Potter
character names and illustrations.

Frederick Warne & Co is the owner of all rights, copyrights and trademarks in the
Beatrix Potter character names and illustrations.

All rights reserved. Without limiting the rights under copyright listed above, no part of this
publication may be reproduced, stored in or introduced into a retrieval system, or transmitted
in any form or by any means (electronic, mechanical, photocopying, recording or otherwise),
without the prior written permission of the above publisher of this book.

ISBN 0 7232 8369 9

Manufactured in China by Imago Publishing Ltd

CONTENTS

THE TALE OF PETER RABBIT
AND BENJAMIN BUNNY.....................7

THE TALE OF TOM KITTEN
AND JEMIMA PUDDLE-DUCK.........................37

THE TALE OF SAMUEL WHISKERS.................67

THE TAILOR OF GLOUCESTER.......................97

The Tale of Peter Rabbit and Benjamin Bunny

Once upon a time there were four little rabbits, and their names were
Flopsy, Mopsy, Cotton-tail and Peter.

They lived with their mother in a sandbank, underneath the root of a
very big fir-tree.

'Now, then,' said Mrs Rabbit one morning to her children, 'you may go
into the fields, or down the lane but don't go into Mr McGregor's garden.
Your father had an accident there - he was put in a pie by Mrs McGregor.'

'Run along now and don't get into mischief. I'm going out,' said Mrs Rabbit.

Then she took her basket and umbrella and went through the wood to the baker.

Flopsy, Mopsy and Cotton-tail, who were good little bunnies, went down the lane to gather blackberries.

10

But Peter, who was very naughty, ran off towards Mr McGregor's garden. On the way he saw his cousin Benjamin.

'Meet me tomorrow - at the big fir tree!' Benjamin whispered.

Peter squeezed under the gate into Mr McGregor's garden.

'Mama will never find out,' he said to himself.

First he ate some lettuces and some French beans; and then he ate some radishes.

'Ooh! My favourite,' he said happily, 'I can't wait to tell Benjamin.'

Peter ate so many radishes that he began to feel rather sick.

'Oh,' he groaned, 'I had better find a little bit of parsley,' and off he went to search for some.

But whom do you think he should meet round the end of a cucumber frame?

'Oh help!' gasped Peter. 'It's Mr McGregor!'

Mr McGregor was planting out young cabbages, but he jumped up and was after Peter in no time, shouting, 'Stop, thief!'

Peter was most dreadfully frightened; he rushed all over the garden, for he had forgotten the way back to the gate. He lost his shoes and ran faster on all fours. Indeed, Peter might have got away altogether if he had not run into a gooseberry net.

'Hurry, Peter, hurry,' urged some friendly sparrows. 'Mr McGregor's coming! Quick, you must keep trying.'

'It's no use,' sobbed Peter trying to struggle free, 'my brass buttons are all caught up.'

Mr McGregor came up with a sieve, which he intended to pop on the top of Peter, but Peter wriggled free leaving his jacket behind him.

He rushed into the toolshed, and jumped into a watering can. It would have been a beautiful thing to hide in if it had not had so much water in it.

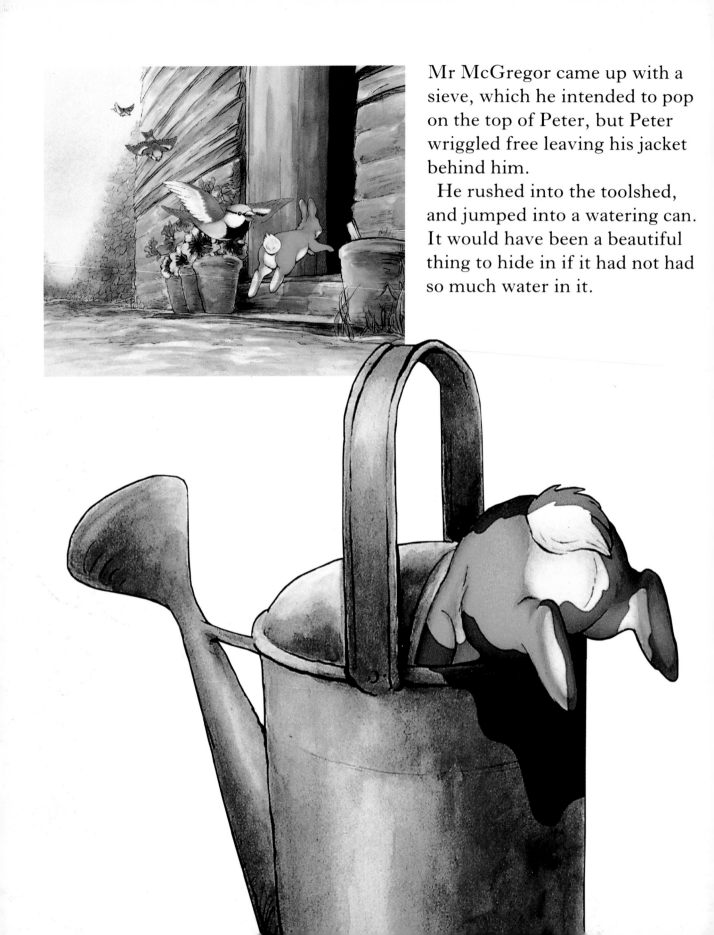

'Come on oot, ye wee beastie -
I know you're here somewhere,'
muttered Mr McGregor,
searching for Peter under the
flower pots.

Suddenly, Peter sneezed,
'Kertyschoo!' and
Mr McGregor was after him in
no time.

Peter jumped out of a window
and ran off.

Peter was quite lost. He found a door in a wall; but it was locked and there was no room for a fat little rabbit to squeeze underneath.

He saw a little old mouse carrying peas to her family.

'If you please, Ma'am, could you tell me the way to the gate?' he asked.

'Mmmm,' was all she could mumble in reply.

'Oh, but which way?' asked Peter sadly, and he began to cry.

Presently, Peter came to a pond where a white cat was staring at some goldfish.

'I must be quiet,' he said to himself. 'Cousin Benjamin has warned me about cats.'

And then Peter saw the gate. He ran as fast as he could, slipped under the gate, and was safe at last in the wood outside the garden.

Mr McGregor hung up the little jacket and the shoes for a scarecrow to frighten the blackbirds.

'Where have you been?' asked Peter's mother. 'And where are your clothes? That is the second little jacket and pair of shoes you've lost in a fortnight. You're to go straight to bed without any supper and I will make you some camomile tea.'

But Flopsy, Mopsy and Cottontail had bread and milk and blackberries for supper.

The next day Benjamin Bunny was sitting on a bank waiting for Peter.
 'Where has Peter got to?' he wondered, when suddenly he heard the trit trot, trit trot of a pony.
 'Well, what luck! It's Mr and Mrs McGregor going out! I'd better find Peter right away,' he thought and rushed off to find his cousin.

Benjamin found Peter sitting alone, wrapped only in a red cotton pocket-handkerchief and looking very sorry for himself.

'I say!' exclaimed Benjamin. 'You do look poorly. Who has got your clothes?'

'The scarecrow in Mr McGregor's garden,' replied Peter and he told Benjamin what had happened the day before.

Benjamin laughed. 'That's what I came to tell you. Mr McGregor has gone out in the gig, *and* Mrs McGregor.'

They made their way to
Mr McGregor's garden and got up
onto the wall. They looked down.
Peter's coat and shoes were plainly
to be seen on the scarecrow, topped
with an old tam-o-shanter of
Mr McGregor's.

'It spoils people's clothes to
squeeze under a gate,' said
Benjamin. 'The *proper* way to get in,
is to climb down a pear tree.'

Little Benjamin said that the first
thing to be done was to get back
Peter's clothes.

There had been rain during the
night; there was water in the shoes
and the coat was somewhat shrunk.

'We can use the handkerchief to carry onions as a present for Aunt,' said Benjamin as they gathered the bundle together.

'Come along Peter,' urged Benjamin.

Peter was not enjoying himself.

Benjamin on the contrary was perfectly at home and ate a lettuce leaf.

Peter did not eat anything and said he should like to go home. Then he dropped half the onions!

But as they turned a corner, Peter and Benjamin stopped suddenly.
'Gracious, what now, Benjamin?' asked Peter.
This is what those little rabbits saw round the corner!

'Quick, under here,' whispered Benjamin. 'She's coming towards us.'

Perhaps the cat liked the smell of onions - because she sat down on top of the basket.

'Now what do we do?' sobbed Peter miserably.

'She'll have to go in for her supper soon,' said Benjamin hopefully.

But the cat slept on the basket for *five hours*.

Mrs Rabbit was getting anxious.

'Mr Bouncer, have you seen my son, Peter? He's been missing all day.'

'Benjamin has taken himself off too,' replied Benjamin's father. 'Leave it to me, ma'am, I think I know where the young rascals have got to. And if I'm right . . .'

'Father!' shouted Benjamin from beneath the basket.

The cat looked up and saw Mr Bouncer prancing along the top of the wall. Mr Bouncer had no opinion whatever of cats and he kicked her into the greenhouse and locked the door.

Mr Bouncer pulled Benjamin from beneath the basket.

'Benjamin first, I think, then Peter . . . Off home with you now.'

Then Mr Bouncer took the handkerchief of onions, and marched those two naughty rabbits all the way home.

When Peter got home his sisters rushed to greet him.

'Well, at least you've found your jacket and shoes, Peter,' said Mrs Rabbit, relieved to see her son home safely.

'There now my dears,' she added, 'all's well that ends well. But let that be a lesson to you, Peter.'

The Tale of
Tom Kitten and
Jemima Puddle-Duck

Once upon a time there were three little kittens, and their names were Mittens, Tom Kitten and Moppet.

They had dear little coats of their own; and they tumbled about the doorstep and played in the dust.

'I do wish Mrs Twitchit would keep her kittens in order,' quacked Jemima Puddle-duck.

One day their mother - Mrs
Tabitha Twitchit - expected friends
to tea; so she fetched her kittens
indoors, to wash and dress them
before her visitors arrived.

First she scrubbed their faces and
then she brushed their fur.

'Stay where you are, you two,' she
warned and she dressed Mittens
and Moppet in clean pinafores.

Then it was Tom's turn.

'Goodness me, Tom, I had not realised quite how much you have grown. Oh dear, oh dear!' sighed Mrs Tabitha Twitchit. 'We'll just have to make the best of it.'

She sewed the buttons back on again, and Tom was squeezed into his best suit.

'Now, keep your frocks clean, children,' said Mrs Tabitha Twitchit.
'You must walk on your hind legs. Keep away from the dirty ash-pit. And
from the pigsty - oh, *and* the Puddle-ducks,' she continued.
  Then she let the kittens out into the garden to be out of the way.

'Let's climb up the rockery, and sit on the
garden wall,' suggested Moppet eagerly.
  Moppet's white tucker fell down into the road.
'Never mind,' she said, 'we can fetch it later.
Now, where's Tom?'
  'He's still down there,' said Mittens, pointing
to the rockery below them.

'Come along, Tom, hurry yourself up,' Mittens called.

Tom was all in pieces when he reached the top of the wall; his hat fell off and the rest of his buttons burst.

While Mittens and Moppet tried to pull him together there was a pit pat paddle-pat! and the three Puddle-ducks came along the road. They stopped and stared up at the kittens. Then they caught sight of the kittens' clothes lying at the bottom of the wall!

'Rather fetching, don't you agree, Jemima?' asked Rebeccah, as she tried on Tom's hat.

Mittens laughed so much that she fell off the wall. Moppet and Tom followed her down.

'Come and help me to dress Tom,' said Moppet to Mr Drake Puddle-duck.

But Mr Drake put Tom's clothes on *himself*.

'It is a very fine morning,' he said and he and Jemima and Rebeccah Puddle-duck set off up the road, keeping step - pit pat, paddle pat!

Then Mrs Tabitha Twitchit came down the garden path and saw her kittens on the wall with no clothes on.

'Oh, my goodness,' she gasped, 'just look at you! My friends will arrive any moment and you are not fit to be seen - I am affronted!

'Straight to your room and not one sound do I wish to hear,' she ordered.

When Mrs Tabitha Twitchit's friends arrived I am sorry to say she told them that her kittens were in bed with the measles; which was not true.

'Dear, dear. What a shame. The poor souls,' exclaimed Henrietta.

But the kittens were not in bed; *not* in the least.

At the tea-party, strange noises were heard from above. 'You did say they were poorly, didn't you, Tabitha dear?' asked Cousin Ribby curiously.

As for the Puddle-ducks, they went into a pond. The clothes all came off because there were no buttons, and they have been looking for them ever since.

Indeed, Jemima was no better at
finding things than she was at
hiding them. She had often tried to
hide her eggs, but they were always
found and carried off. No-one
believed that Jemima had the
patience to sit on her eggs.

  Poor Jemima became quite
desperate.

'I *will* hatch my own eggs, if I have to make a nest right away from the farm,' she said.

So, one fine spring afternoon, Jemima put on her best bonnet and shawl and set off.

Jemima landed in a clearing in the middle of a wood. She began to waddle about in search of a nesting place, when suddenly she was startled to find an elegantly dressed gentleman reading a newspaper.

'Madam, have you lost your way?' he enquired politely.

'Oh, no,' Jemima explained. 'I am trying to find a convenient, dry nesting place so that I may sit on my eggs.'

54

'Is that so? Indeed! How interesting! As to a nest there is no difficulty: I have a sackful of feathers in my wood-shed,' said the bushy long-tailed gentleman. He opened the door to show Jemima.

  'You will be in nobody's way. You may sit there as long as you like,' he assured her.

'Goodness,' thought Jemima, 'I've never seen so many feathers in one place. Very comfortable, though, and perfect for making my nest, so warm . . . so dry.'

The sandy-whiskered gentleman promised to take great care of Jemima's nest until she came back again the next day.

'Nothing I love better than eggs and ducklings. I should be proud to see a fine nestful in my wood-shed. Oh, what would be a finer sight?'

Jemima Puddle-duck came every afternoon, and laid nine eggs in the nest. The foxy gentleman admired them immensely.

At last Jemima told the gentleman she was ready to sit on her eggs until they hatched.

'Madam,' he said, 'before you commence your tedious sitting I intend to give you a treat. Let us have a dinner party all to ourselves. May I ask you to bring some herbs from the farm garden to make, er . . . a savoury omelette? I will provide lard for the stuffing . . . I mean, omelette.'

Jemima Puddle-duck was a simpleton; she quite unsuspectingly went round nibbling snippets off all the different sorts of herbs that are used for stuffing roast duck.

'What are you doing with those onions?' asked Kep, the collie dog. 'And where do you go every afternoon by yourself?'

Jemima told him the whole story.

'Now, exactly where is your nest?' enquired Kep suspiciously.

Jemima went up the cart-road for the last time and flew over the wood.

When she arrived the bushy long-tailed gentleman was waiting for her.

'Come into the house just as soon as you've looked at your eggs,' he ordered sharply. Jemima had never heard him speak like that. She felt surprised and uncomfortable.

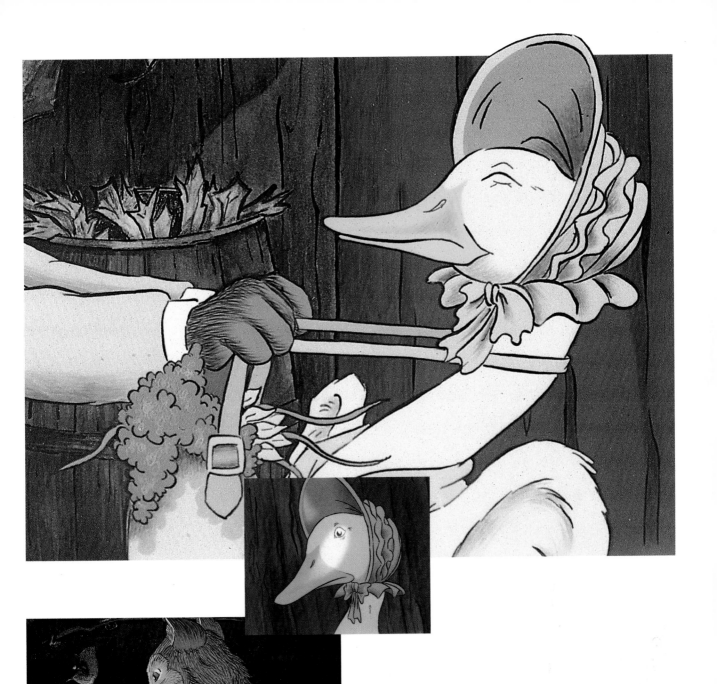

While Jemima was inside she heard pattering feet round the back of the shed. She became much alarmed.

'Oh, what shall I do?' she worried.

A moment afterwards there were the most awful noises - barking, growls and howls, squealing and groans.

'And I think that is the last we will
see of that foxy-whiskered
gentleman,' said Kep.

Unfortunately the puppies had gobbled up all of Jemima's eggs before Kep could stop them.

'There, there, Jemima,' comforted Kep, 'I'm afraid it's just in the nature of things - best make our way home to the farmyard, where you belong, my dear.'

Poor Jemima Puddle-duck was escorted home.

Jemima laid some more eggs in June and she was allowed to keep them herself; but only four of them hatched. She said that it was because of her nerves, but she had always been a bad sitter.

THE TALE OF
SAMUEL WHISKERS

Once upon a time there was an old cat, called Mrs Tabitha Twitchit, who was an anxious parent. She used to lose her kittens continually, and whenever they were lost they were always in mischief!

On baking day Mrs Tabitha Twitchit determined to shut her kittens in a cupboard.

'And there you stay my two young rascals, until my baking is finished,' she said to Moppet and Mittens.

But she could not find Tom.

Tom Kitten did *not* want to be shut in a cupboard, so he looked around for a convenient place to hide and fixed upon the chimney.

Inside the chimney, Tom coughed and choked with the smoke. He began to climb right to the top.

'I cannot go back. If I slipped I might fall in the fire and singe my beautiful tail and my little blue jacket,' he said.

While Mrs Tabitha Twitchit was searching for Tom, Moppet and Mittens pushed open the cupboard door. They went straight to the dough which was set to rise in a pan in front of the fire.

'Shall we make dear little muffins?' said Mittens to Moppet.

But just at that moment, somebody knocked at the door, and a voice called out: 'Tabitha! Are you at home, Tabitha?'

'Oh, come in Cousin Ribby. I'm in sad trouble. I've lost my dear son Thomas. I'm afraid the rats have got him,' sobbed Mrs Tabitha Twitchit. 'And now Moppet and Mittens are gone too. What it is to have an unruly family,' she wailed.

'Well Cousin, we shan't find any of them standing here,' said Ribby firmly. 'I'm not afraid of rats. I'll help you find Tom - and whip him too. Now, just where would a naughty kitten hide?'

Meanwhile, up the chimney Tom Kitten was getting very frightened! It was confusing in the dark, and he felt quite lost.

All at once he fell head over heels
down a hole and landed on a heap of
very dirty rags.

'What a peculiar smell,' said Tom
Kitten to himself. 'It's something
like a mouse . . . only dreadfully
strong . . . Oh!' he gasped suddenly.

Opposite to him - as far away as he
could sit - was an enormous rat.

'What do you mean by tumbling into my bed all covered with smuts?'
asked the rat (whose name was Samuel Whiskers).

  'Please sir, the chimney wants sweeping,' said poor Tom Kitten
miserably.

'Anna Maria! Anna Maria!' Samuel Whiskers called.
  There was a pattering noise and an old woman rat poked her head
round a rafter.

'What have we here, Samuel?' she asked. 'A tasty morsel indeed!' She rushed upon Tom and before he knew what was happening, he was rolled up in a bundle, and tied with string in very tight knots.

'Anna Maria,' said the old man rat,
'make me a kitten dumpling
roly-poly pudding for my dinner.'

'Hmm . . . it requires dough and a pat of butter and a rolling-pin,'
said Anna Maria.
 The two rats consulted together for a few minutes and then went away.

Samuel Whiskers went boldly down the front staircase to the dairy to get the butter.

He made a second journey for the rolling-pin, which he pushed in front of him with his paws.

82

Anna Maria went to the kitchen to steal the dough. She borrowed a small saucer, and scooped up the dough with her paws.

'He is rather a large kitten for his age,' she muttered, as she scooped up another pawful.

Presently the rats came back and set to work to make Tom Kitten into a dumpling. First they smeared him with butter, and then they rolled him in the dough.

Ribby and Mrs Tabitha Twitchit heard a curious roly-poly noise under the attic floor, but there was nothing to be seen so they returned to the kitchen. Ribby found Moppet hiding in a flour barrel.

'Moppet!' scolded Mrs Twitchit.

'But mother,' cried Moppet, 'there's been an old woman rat in the kitchen and she's stolen some of the dough!'

Mittens was found in the dairy, hiding in an empty jar.

'There's been an old man rat in the dairy, mother. He's stolen a pat of butter and a rolling-pin!' Mittens cried.

'Oh my poor son, Thomas!' exclaimed Tabitha, wringing her paws.

Ribby and Mrs Tabitha Twitchit rushed upstairs. Sure enough, the roly-poly noise was still going on quite distinctly under the attic floor.

'Oh my goodness, this is serious, Cousin Tabitha,' said Ribby. 'We must send for John Joiner at once, with a saw.'

And what was happening to Tom Kitten? All this time, the two rats had
been hard at work.

'Will not the string be very indigestible, Anna Maria?' inquired Samuel
Whiskers.

'No, no, no. It is of no consequence,' she replied before turning to Tom.
'I do wish you would stop moving your head about. It disarranges the
dough so.'

'Oh, Mr Joiner, this way,' said Cousin Ribby. 'We can hear the strangest sounds . . . I dread to think! Come along, follow me quickly now.'

'I do *not* think it will be a good pudding,' said Samuel Whiskers, looking at Tom Kitten. 'It smells sooty.'

Anna Maria was about to argue the point, when they heard noises up above - the rasping of a saw, and the noise of a little dog, scratching and yelping!

'We are discovered and interrupted, Anna Maria. Let us collect our property (and other people's) and depart at once. I fear that we shall be obliged to leave this pudding, but I am persuaded that the knots would have proved indigestible,' said Samuel Whiskers.

So it happened that by the time
John Joiner had got the plank up
there was nobody under the
floor except the rolling-pin and
Tom Kitten in a very dirty
dumpling!

Samuel Whiskers and Anna Maria found a wheelbarrow belonging to Miss Potter which they borrowed and hastily filled with a quantity of bundles.

'There may just have been room for the pudding,' said Samuel Whiskers wistfully.

'I notice that *you* are not pushing the barrow,' retorted Anna Maria. 'You might be of another opinion if you were!'

Then Samuel Whiskers and Anna Maria made their way to Farmer Potatoes' hay barn and hauled their parcels with a bit of string to the top of the hay mow.

'Be quick,' urged Anna Maria, 'and tie the bundles on, or Miss Potter will be missing the barrow.'

The cat family quickly recovered. The dumpling was peeled off Tom
Kitten and made separately into a pudding, with currants in it to hide the
smuts. They had to put Tom Kitten into a hot bath to get the butter off.
  And after that, there were no more rats for a long time at Mrs Tabitha
Twitchit's.

THE TAILOR OF GLOUCESTER

In the time of swords and periwigs and full-skirted coats with flowered lappets - when gentlemen wore ruffles and gold-laced waistcoats of paduasoy and taffeta - there lived a tailor in Gloucester.

He sat in the window of a little shop in Westgate Street, cross-legged on a table, from morning till night.

One bitter cold day near Christmas, the tailor began to make a coat of cherry-coloured corded silk.

'The finest of wedding-coats for the Mayor of Gloucester who is to be married on Christmas Day in the morning,' he muttered to himself as he worked.

The table was all littered with cherry-coloured snippets.

'I'm sure I cannot afford to waste the smallest piece,' said the tailor as he continued cutting. 'Too narrow breadths for nought except waistcoats for mice!

   'Now, the lining . . . Ah yes! Just the thing - yellow taffeta.'

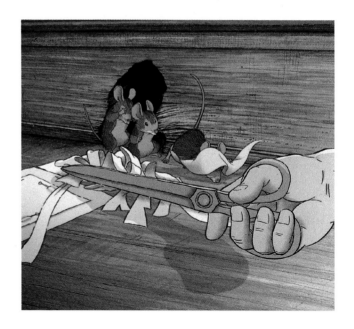

Unnoticed, little mice retrieved the scraps from his work bench and carried them off.

'By my whiskers, I cannot remember when we had silk of such quality on these premises!' exclaimed the little mouse.

'Oh, yellow taffeta - just what I would have chosen myself,' whispered another.

'My poor back,' sighed the tailor, 'but it is done. The light is fading and I am tired. All is ready to sew in the morning, except for one item - I am wanting one single skein of cherry-coloured twisted silk thread.'

The old tailor locked up his shop and shuffled home through the snow.

The mice were more fortunate and did not have to brave the cold. Using secret passages and staircases behind the wooden wainscots of all the old houses in Gloucester, they could run from house to house.

The tailor lived alone with his cat, whose name was Simpkin. All day long, while the tailor was out at work, Simpkin kept house by himself. Simpkin was also fond of the mice, but he gave them no satin for coats!

'Ah, Simpkin, old friend!' exclaimed the tailor as he arrived home. 'We shall make our fortune from this coat, but I am worn to a ravelling. Now, take this groat (which is our last fourpence) and buy a penn'orth of bread, a penn'orth of milk and a penn'orth of sausages.'

'And, Simpkin,' remembered the tailor, 'with the last penny of our fourpence buy me one penn'orth of cherry-coloured silk. But do *not* lose the last penny, Simpkin, or I am undone and worn to a thread-paper, for I have *no more twist*.'

The tailor was very tired and beginning to be ill. He sat by the hearth and talked to himself about that wonderful coat.

'The Mayor has ordered a coat and an embroidered waistcoat to be lined with yellow taffeta.'

Suddenly, interrupting him, were a number of little noises coming from the dresser at the other side of the kitchen - *Tip tap, tip tap tip!*

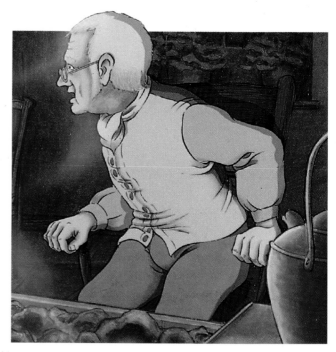

Tip tap, tip tap tip!

'Now what can that be?' the tailor wondered. He crossed the kitchen, and stood quite still beside the dresser, listening and peering through his spectacles.

Tip tap, tip tap, tip tap tip!

The tailor lifted up a teacup which was upside-down. Out stepped a little live lady mouse. Then, out from under teacups and from under bowls and basins, stepped more little mice.

'Good gracious, this is very peculiar,' remarked the tailor. 'I'll wager this is all Simpkin's doing, the rascal.

'Oh, was I wise to entrust my last fourpence to Simpkin? And was it right to let loose those mice, undoubtedly the property of Simpkin?'

Simpkin returned and opened the
door with an angry 'G-r-r-miaw!'
like a cat that is vexed: for he hated
the snow, and there was snow in his
ears, and snow in his collar at the
back of his neck.

He sniffed and then looked
suspiciously at the dresser - the
cups and jugs had been moved!
Simpkin wanted his supper of a
little fat mouse.

'Simpkin,' asked the tailor
anxiously, 'where is my *twist*?'

Simpkin was cross with his master,
and if he had been able to talk he would have asked:
'Where is my *mouse*?'
  He quickly hid the twist in the teapot on the dresser,
and growled at the tailor.
  'Where is my twist, Simpkin? Alack, I am undone. . . I am so weak,'
lamented the tailor and went sadly to bed.

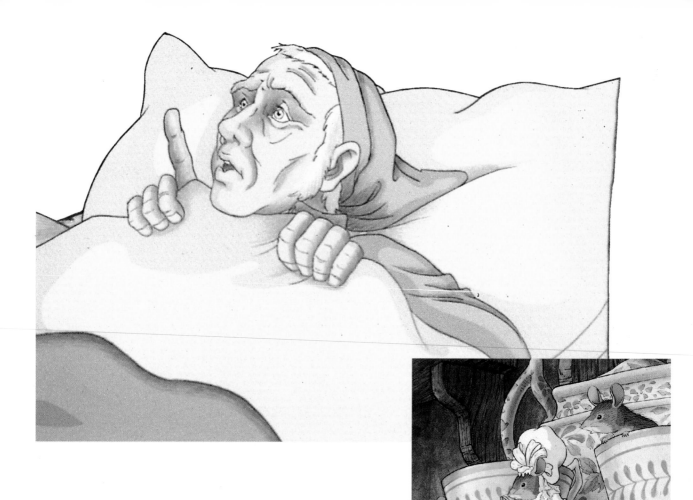

The poor old tailor was very ill with fever, tossing and turning in his four-post bed; and still in his dreams he mumbled - 'No more twist. . . one-and-twenty buttonholes. . . to be finished by noon on Saturday . . . and it is already Tuesday!'

The little mice came out again, and listened to the tailor; and they took notice of the pattern of that wonderful coat. They whispered to one another about the taffeta lining, and about little mouse tippets.

Indeed, what should become of the cherry-coloured coat?

In the tailor's shop the embroidered silk and satin lay cut out upon the table, and who should come to sew them when the window was barred and the door was fast locked?

The tailor lay ill for three days and three nights and then it was Christmas Eve and very late at night. The moon climbed up over the roofs and chimneys. All the city of Gloucester was fast asleep under the snow.

The cathedral clock struck twelve and Simpkin went out into the night.

For an old story tells how all the animals can talk in the night between Christmas Eve and Christmas Day in the morning (though very few people can hear them, or know what it is that they say).

Simpkin wandered through the streets feeling lonely and hungry.

'My master's cupboard is as empty as old Mother Hubbard's,' he complained miserably.

But when Simpkin turned a corner he saw a glow of light coming from the tailor's shop. He crept up to peep in at the window.

Inside the shop was a
snippeting of scissors and a
snappeting of thread and
little mouse voices were
singing loudly and happily:
'Three little mice sat down
  to spin,
Pussy passed by and she
  peeped in.'

Simpkin miaowed to get in but the door was locked.

'Dear me, and the key is under the tailor's pillow,' mocked a little mouse seamstress gleefully.

Simpkin came away from the shop and went home. There he found the poor old tailor without fever, sleeping peacefully.

Then Simpkin went on tip-toe and took a little parcel of silk out of the teapot - he felt quite ashamed of his badness compared with those good little mice!

When the tailor awoke the next morning, the first thing which he saw upon the patchwork quilt, was a skein of cherry-coloured twisted silk, and beside it the repentant Simpkin!

The tailor got up and dressed and went out into the street.

'I have my twist,' he said to himself, 'but no more strength nor time than will serve to make me one single buttonhole; for this is Christmas Day in the morning! The Mayor of Gloucester is to be married by noon - and where is his cherry-coloured coat?'

He unlocked the door of the little shop and looked in amazement.

There, where he had left plain cuttings of silk now lay the most beautiful coat and embroidered satin waistcoat that ever were worn by a Mayor of Gloucester!

Everything was finished except for one single cherry-coloured buttonhole, and where that buttonhole was wanting there was pinned a scrap of paper with these words - in little teeny weeny writing - NO MORE TWIST.

And from then began the luck of the Tailor of Gloucester; he grew quite stout, and he grew quite rich.

Never were seen such ruffles, or such embroidered cuffs. But his buttonholes were the greatest triumph - the stitches were *so* neat and *so* small they looked as if they had been made by little mice!